"House of D'Antonio"

by

Reece Cooper James

HOUSE OF D'ANTONIO

REECE COOPER
JAMES

Library of Congress Control Number: 2016955381

ISBN: 978-0-9776377-8-2
Printed in the United States of America
First Printing

Cover design by The Liar's Craft

For more information or to order additional
books, please contact:
Black Angle Publishers
P.O. Box 2974
Upper Marlboro, MD 20773
www.blackanglepub.com

Prologue

In the middle of her freshman year at the university, Abi moved out of the crowded dorm room for a quieter one in a boarding house three miles from the main campus. There, she had more privacy and could study without constant interruption from the freshmen goof-offs. She took her studies far more seriously than the average student, and at the age of sixteen, compared to the other girls, Abi was mature beyond her years. By now, her business was well established, and between it and her studies, she had little time for idle chitchat. Before her final business class, she gathered her toiletries and walked the short distance to the shower facilities at the opposite end of the hallway. After looking around, she was relieved to know that she was the only one in the two-man (or in this case, woman) shower area. She stepped in and adjusted the water temperature. Abi positioned her body directly under the massive rain showerhead, raised her head to allow the flow of the water to pulsate onto her face and down her body. She stood there motionless, enjoying the euphoric feeling the warmth of the water allowed her tired body to feel, a peacefulness she hadn't enjoyed since enrolling in the university. Abi inhaled a deep breath before exhaling sharply, making a sound as she did. Once she took her next breath, a familiar scent invaded her space. It was a scent, although familiar, that she hadn't smelled in quite some time. Abi was frozen – unable to move. Opening her eyes, she looked around the steamy enclosure, sensing a watchful eye peering in her direction. There was no one in sight, but she could still feel someone's dominating presence. Abi tried to reach for the shower gel and loofah but was unable to do so. She couldn't move. Somewhere and somehow, time seemed to have stopped. The water from the showerhead paused in mid-air – not a drop of water seeped through the holes. Abi could neither look up nor down, only straight ahead at the white ceramic walls of the shower. It was as if she were in suspended animation. But the one sense she still possessed was her smell of that scent from many years before. The one she pinned for her make-believe friend. This time, it appeared stronger, as if whoever wore it was standing directly in front of her. She tried to open her mouth to scream, but even that part of her was immobile. Suddenly, it dawned on her that her friend, the one friend she had not talked to in quite some time, was here with her. Her imaginary friend, Roman

D'Antonio, had made his presence without being summoned. He was there, with her, staring at her. He, Roman D'Antonio, was the reason time stood still. That's when she felt his touch on the side of her cheek. He slid it down her face onto her neck, and then her chest, where it rested on her breast. He had never touched her; he had no reason to do so because he was in her mind. She summoned him whenever she needed him. Not the other way around. For what seemed like hours, he skillfully massaged and played with her breasts, one after the other. Abi wanted to scream or let out a cry for help, but no sound could escape her. Then suddenly he entered her – she gasped or thought she had made a sound. Her body began to respond to the foreign, faceless apparition violating her. Abi could feel her mouth quivering; her eyes blinked rapidly; moisture formed in the corners of both. Her body shook from the internal pleasure provided by her imaginary friend, the phantom she named Roman D'Antonio. Then suddenly, when she thought her body could no longer endure the overwhelming pleasure of this invasive act, she was lifted from the floor and hurled to the back of the shower wall. Her limp body slid down the wall until it collapsed on the warm wet floor. Abi watched in awe as the shower water returned to its normal pulsating pattern, falling onto her limp frame. Her imaginary friend just violated the code of conduct between dreamer and her dreams – he made his debut by performing a non-consensual sex act on her untouched passage.

Chapter i

The mid-15th century brought about turmoil,
which was the way of the land for many warriors.
during that time period. Located in the middle of
the North Sea, Brocklehurst Island had no
democracy or order, though many native
warriors made attempts at ruling the land. These
warriors attempted to stake their claim to rule
through battle and even death. All attempts to
fully control the Kingdom of Brocklehurst failed
until the family of Asethemis arose. With over

twenty heads, countless warriors, and alluringly beautiful maidens, they made their mark. Every warrior was prepared to battle the inhabitants and the skilled maidens were well practiced, successfully used to entice the weak-minded of the land.

In the year 1464, the families of Asethemis and Nathegio were brought together by marriage. The widower King Bertram of Asethemis sought out the beautiful Margaret, fourteen-year-old princess to the Nathegio throne. Therefore a truce between the two houses was formed, birthing the House of D'Antonio.

Twenty years later, with six surviving

children, Margaret found herself sitting on the throne awaiting the coronation of her thirteen-year-old son, Remington. Her husband had suffered a horrible death after being poisoned by one of his cooks, who in turn met his fate by public beheading. Prince Remington, the first of two male heirs, would soon be crowned king. Even though Remington had six sisters, the throne should have gone to Margaret II, but she was married to the bastard son of George III, Lord York of Yorkster, Gaston, who had become the number-one enemy of Queen Margaret's brother, Edmund III. Edmund detested his niece's husband because he had suspected

Gaston of treason to the throne long before the death of the King. Edmund always thought that Gaston was the reason for the demise of his own father, Edmund II. So he intended to prevent Gaston from taking over his late brother-in-law's kingdom, and he sought the assistance of the parliament. Weeks after the King's death, Parliament ruled that no bastard child shall ever rule the kingdom of D'Antonio.

Gaston did not take the ruling kindly, so he left the kingdom taking Edmund's niece, Margaret II, and his two young sons for Yorkster. Margaret II had to leave behind fortunes in land, jewelry, and valuable coins, all willed to her because of her royal heritage. Margaret II was not happy leaving her mother and uncle, but because of her loyalty, she honored her husband's wishes. Although penniless and with only the royal blood of Margaret and their sons, the Duke of Yorkster welcomed his cousin and made sure that the family was taken care of.

Not long after settling in Yorkster, Gaston was bestowed Duke of Yorkster, but that title didn't last long. Many thought he was unworthy to hold such an honor, and therefore Gaston had gained enemies – the same enemies who planned his untimely death.

After the death of her husband, Margaret II

prepared to return to the kingdom of D'Antonio with her now ten-year-old son George IV and twelve-year-old Gaston II. However, before she could gather her belongings, her uncle got word to her that she and her sons were no longer welcome in the D'Antonio kingdom. Hearing this news, Lord Yorkster promised Margaret lands and riches of her own if she would wed her son Gaston II with his granddaughter, Lady Carol. She agreed. A few years later Gaston, with Carol and their son, Gaston III, travelled away from Yorkster, not able to control the shame of being ridiculed by the natives because of his family's exile from their native land. He wanted nothing to do with the Yorkster throne. Gaston's family was never to be heard of again.

Chapter ii

When Abigail was at the tender age of six, her parents, Clarita and Thaddeus Trenaulde, couldn't reconcile years of differences, and after many nights of disagreements, finally decided that the only solution was to part ways. The only decision the two could agree on was which parent would raise which child. In lieu of joint parenting, the two decided that Lamarnd would be raised by Thaddeus – after all, the young preteen needed to be raised by his father. Young Abi was left in the care of their unstable mother. After the separation, Abi had no idea that it would mean the division of her and her brother.

Lamarnd, or Mardi as she referred lovingly to him, was her savior. Seven years her senior, he was her only playmate as her mother did not allow her to own any toys: no doll babies, no teddy bears, no tea sets, and worst of all, no friends to play with. In between the seriousness of the family business, she and Mardi would sneak in time for play. Even though playtime was disallowed, they somehow managed. Abi's most memorable moments were the times she would sneak in his bedroom at the top of the stairs and jump up and down on his bed until he would catch her small frame in mid-air. If she giggled too loud, her mother would storm in the room and separate the two. She worshipped the ground Mardi walked on, and from an early age, he was her playmate, her buddy and best friend forever – so she thought. The separation tore a huge wedge in not only her life but her soul as well. Abi needed her older brother to guide her through life, but that closeness they once shared was suddenly disrupted after the demise of their parent's union. She replayed in her mind the day he left.

"Promise me you'll keep in touch." Abi's tiny

voice pleaded in between uncontrollable sobs.

"I promise. I'll call you every day," he told her and then added, "Remember, you have more power than you know – be careful with it."

"Okay." But she had no idea what his final words meant. She had always been told of the powers the family possessed during the nightly rituals, but as a child didn't know how to put them to good use.

Abi's daily routine was to wake up, have breakfast with the family, study, eat dinner with the family, and participate in psychosomatic chants or better known as Divining.in the small dark den. This is how the family connects with and further enhances their metaphysics with the underworld. Abi enjoyed these moments with the family because each time, her perception of the other dimensions increased. She could mind-travel to different places and each travel was always an ecstatic experience; an experience her soul could never feel any other way.

Her mother hid the fact that she and her husband had conflicting views about their nightly Divining chants. He was more determined to stay connected to his ancestors by frequently projecting himself back in time. She on the other hand showed little interest in continuing any family feud that should have been laid to rest long after the wars many years prior. Her mother wanted to remain planted in this one dimension of time. She was fearful of the unknown. But Abi's father was a warrior from childhood; he was a master at projecting his soul from his physical body to transport through time. He shared many stories with her and her brother.

Abi's father prided himself in the unique heritage his ancestors handed down. During their nightly chants, he told them of how many years ago, their family was run out of the kingdom because of an illegal marriage. Her father would remind them of the royal blood that ran through them. He explained how his ancestor placed a curse on the king of a mighty land. Thaddeus always feared some form of retaliation from the king's ancestors, but after many years, the Trenaulde family remained safe.

"One day," her father began, "you will need what was handed down to you by our ancestors. As you grow, you will learn how and when to use The Craft." Abi was much too young to comprehend the seriousness of his claim, so she ignored it, as would any young child.

On that sad day, she watched the vehicle pull out of the driveway, leaving her standing alone on the cold pavement. Her mother never bothered to see them off. Abi's world was shattered on this day as she felt abandoned.

Little did she know that Mardi's decision to live with their father meant all communication between the two would be severed. Years later, she discovered that their mother intercepted his phone calls, refusing to allow the two siblings to communicate. Once again, her world was turned upside down. At that time, it was unknown why Clarita was a bitter, unhappy woman and chose to remove herself and Abi from the world.

As she matured, Abi learned the real reason behind her mother's reclusive behavior and why her father left the home. Clarita couldn't rid herself of divine consciousness – her belief was centered on the mortal beings, which is why Thaddeus left the home. Abi was left with a miserable, self-centered, woman who claimed to those outside of the family to be a loving mother. Clarita Trenaulde deprived Abi of the love she yearned for and was alienated from after the abandonment by her father and brother. Eventually her mother withdrew completely from Abi. Clarita didn't know how to parent a growing pre-teen and soon teenager who perfected The Craft better than she. Soon, this alienation had no affect on Abi. She continued to improve on the nightly rituals so that she could better perfect her skills. She knew that one day she would soon need The Craft to protect her from the unknown.

Just like Mardi, Abi was home-schooled her entire life, only interacting with adults outside of her family when school administrators came in the home to either view their arranged classroom settings and to administer exams. Oftentimes, she wanted to plead for them to take her away from this depressing environment. She thought that by ignoring them, they would somehow get the hint that she was unhappy. Each time her silent pleas were ignored.

What little solace she did have was being able to play on the computer. Her mother had restrictions set where she blocked certain access and web pages. She only allowed Abi to do her schoolwork using the application installed by the school officials. But Abi was smart and was able to override those restrictions. For five hours a day, she had access to anything she could find on the Internet, which is how she gained extensive knowledge of the ins-and-outs of the computer environment. Of course, after her schoolwork was completed, Abi would reset those restrictions so that Clarita wouldn't discover her secret.

By the time she was a teenager, she had all the necessary classes to graduate from high school, and when she did, Abi did not hesitate to emancipate herself from her parents and leave her miserable home. She had already secured a dormitory room at the university far away and could move in at any time. On Abi's last day in the Trenaulde home, Clarita locked herself inside the master bedroom, refusing to see her only daughter leave the family home. Abi was thrilled to pack up her few belongings but deep down inside was saddened that no one really cared whether she stayed or not.

Chapter iii

He was whoever she wanted him to be, Roman – her imaginary friend. After the departure of her older brother and father, she invented a replacement. The creation of Roman slowly eased the loneliness she experienced by being the only child in the Trenaulde household, the only six-year-who couldn't play with toys; the only six-year-old who was never allowed to have playdates, which was why Roman was so important to her. He was what she needed to ease the solitude. Their daily conversations were endless. Day in and out, Abi would summon his presence into existence, and like the faithful friend he was, Roman would satisfy the playful antics of this six-year-old. She could summon Roman and talk about things no one seemed to understand – not even her own mother. Abi hosted fake tea parities with her friend. She even had frequent sleepovers. Years later, Roman was her sounding board; she bounced future ideas off of him, and when he agreed, through their secret telepathic passage, she set the wheels in motion.

While she should have been doing schoolwork, Abi created fun things to do on the computer. These fun things became games that were the starting point for Trenaulde Technology. Her Gaming Division designed games for the online community. Soon, she designed learning software first for young children and then for teens. Trenaulde Technology soon created its K-12 Division which included education software for all school age children.

As she grew older, Roman should have been a passing memory, but he continued to be as important in her life as a teenager as he was when she first invented him. Roman became a silent partner in her business ventures. It was he who suggested that she research and develop the Assistive Technology software, which is now one of the more busiest divisions. The older she got, the more real Roman became. On a few occasions, Roman wouldn't just appear when she thought him into presence; minutes after lying awake at night, Abi could feel him hovering over her bed, many times without her even summoning his presence. Once, in her bedroom, she awakened from a deep sleep only to see an apparition standing over her bed. But as she rubbed the sleep from her eyes, and opened them, he, it, that thing was gone. Gone, but the smell of him, it, that thing remained. Roman now had his own unique smell. She wondered if it was even a real scent – or did she simply envision it into existence as she had him? Either way, it was an exclusive odor that she deemed the smell now belonged to Roman. It had a masculine fragrance similar to the earthy smell of freshly cut grass on a midsummer's morning. Her eyes searched the room – she could feel his lingering presence, or there was a spiritual being hovering, staring – someone, something was there. He was there, not only in her imagination, he was there – physically – Roman was there with her, and now he was the one in charge of determining when to appear and when not to. Abi was no longer in command of beckoning her imaginary friend into existence. Knowing this should have frightened her, but he was her invention, and as her invention, Roman was harmless. He was there for guidance, as her brother and father should have been. He was there to teach her life survival skills, skills she should have learned from being a normal child. But Abi was not a normal child, as she grew to realize; she had congenital skills bestowed upon her before she was born and her parents, especially her father made sure that those skills were perfected. Abi was aware that she had to be careful with her special talents, which was why it was necessary for Roman to be there for her. He was her mentor. Somehow she knew Roman D'Antonio would be more than what she originally dreamed him to be.

Chapter iv

Abigail Trenaulde earned her first million before the age of eighteen. When she was a ninth grader, she started Trenaulde Technology, a computer company in her parents' home. By the end of her high school senior year, she had twenty online employees—most were gamers eager to create the next big game application. At the tender age of twenty-five, she had acquired two smaller technology companies, incorporated her business, and was publicly trading on the stock market. Trenaulde Technology gained its respect in the computer world after selling a few infantry computer games to some major software game companies. Today, Abi has achieved what most entrepreneurs' only dream of in such a short time. Abi never had a boyfriend in high school because being home schooled, she didn't attend a traditional school, but most importantly, she had Roman Abi was also fascinated with building an empire. In college, it was more of the same, but her skills had advanced to designing applications and then selling them to larger companies. Trenaulde Technology sales doubled the first year when they started the applications division. Now, Abi no longer ran the company hands-on. She had a full staff, including a chief executive officer who could oversee the daily operations of the business. Her primary focus was building the Software Development division of the company. Delroy Myers, her CEO was instrumental in overseeing any possible ideas either existing or not. His latest project led him to the Atlanta Electronic Expo. Delroy was excited to learn of a company that had designed a new anti-virus software and was the hottest talk in the computer world. Apparently, their product exceeded that of the current anti-virus software by far. Delroy was eager to report back to Abi as he had learned that the owner of this virus software had a planned meeting with a rival company. After that bit of news, Abi wanted to secure a meeting with him so as not to lose out on this potentially important opportunity to further grow her company. She even expensed his flight and hotel.

She looked at her watch for the third time. Three minutes before the start of one of most important meetings on her schedule, Abi had walked into the reception area to await the last guest.

"We checked his itinerary; his flight came in last night on schedule." the receptionist, paused and looked up at a nervous Abi Trenaulde. "It's still early," she reassured her.

Abi stared at the young lady before stating, "If he's not walking through that door in five minutes or less, call his office." Abi handed her a business card retrieved from the portfolio. At that moment, Delroy joined her in the reception area.

"Abi, be patient. He knows how important this meeting is to both companies. We can do a lot for DP Tech and they can do a lot for us." he stated and then added, "so please relax.

The double-glass door to the office opened. He stood there talking quietly on his cellular phone while holding an attaché case in the other hand. Abi hadn't expected someone so young. She thought, *he appears no older than thirty-five. Must have been sent as a representative. Great. They send me a junior-level executive.*

Both the receptionist and Abi watched him as he walked in, oblivious to his surroundings. He was dressed in a black suit, crisp white button down shirt, solid tie and nice, shiny, black unscruffed shoes. He turned to observe his surroundings. Abi stared into the face of the stranger. His honey brown complexion was flawless. His lashes had a perfect curl. She smiled, unable to look away. His presence was demanding, which caught her by surprise. She blinked but still maintained eye contact. He smiled, showing off his perfectly white teeth. He ended his conversation, tucked the cell phone inside his suit pocket, and walked in their direction. The receptionist looked from Abi to him. Clearly, the two were mesmerized with each other. Abi held onto the large planner, clutching it closely to her chest as if protecting it from harm.

The office of Trenaulde Technology was nestled at the entrance of the busy but noisy metro station. Before entering the office space, he reached inside of his coat pocket to retrieve the oversized wedding band. *I'm here only for business.* He reminded himself.

"*I hope this is Miss A. Trenaulde. She is nice looking*," Palmer Stafford thought.

"Good morning, I'm Palmer Stafford of DP Tech. I'm here for the Trenaulde presentation." He extended his manicured hands. When their hands touched, Abi couldn't help but notice his were warm. She thought, *what a nice smile*. She couldn't help but stare. *Not bad for a mere mortal*. She quickly reminded herself the purpose of his being there. She noticed his tall frame, about six feet. His hair was closely trimmed, with thin sideburns trailing down his chiselled jawbone. He had a thin goatee. He was also sporting a wedding band.

Delroy took a step forward, extending his hand. "Good seeing you again Palmer." Then he turned to Abi.

"Hello, I'm Abigail Trenaulde, pleased to meet you." She inhaled his fragrance. The soft scent was fresh as if recently applied. It was Diesel. Because it was a popular fragrance worn by most men, she'd recognize that smell anywhere. Abi had a deep admiration for men who took special care in their appearance and the cologne they wore. She considered herself an expert because the scent she invented for her imaginary friend was just as masculine as the one she was now enjoying.

"Likewise, but call me Palmer."

"Sure, you can call me Abi." She reached for his forearm. "Would you follow me into the conference room? We have a large group anxiously waiting to begin the presentation."

Once the two walked in the room, Abi closed the door and introduced the remaining member to the group. "Have a seat." She pointed in the direction of the only two vacant seats around the extra long oak wood table. After the greetings, Abi opened the meeting with a brief overview of the company but soon turned over the microphone to Delroy, her CEO.

"The Trenaulde effort that will bring the technology..." Abi smiled while taking the empty seat next to Palmer. She could feel his eyes scanning her body.

After two hours of displaying financial statements, flipping through large graphs projected on the screen, and answering questions, the meeting was finally adjourned. Abi was hopping that this meeting would be only the start of either a successful buyout or a negotiation to add DP Tech's anti-virus software Virso Pro to Trenaulde Technology's Software Development Division. Abi gathered her papers and watched the invited group of men and women mingle amongst themselves. She took this moment to reflect. *Everyone seemed happy with what Trenaulde Technology was offering; it was in fact a lucrative offer for DP Tech. I just hope Palmer is smart enough to see it my way*

—

55

instead of considering any other offers he may have received. If all goes as planned, the software development division should be up and running before the end of the year—with or without Palmer. But I need his Virso Pro software rights, which would be a solid start-up project.

"That was very impressive." Palmer interrupted her thoughts. She smiled.

"My CEO is the best in this business. I should know. I recruited heavily to bring him onboard. Besides, I only employ people who are as passionate in the success of the company as I, Palmer."

"When I met Delroy at the expo, he spoke highly of the company and you as well. I was a bit doubtful about coming here today. But after hearing about the Trenaulde Technology way of doing business, I might say you may have swayed my opinion."

"Thank you, sir. We do stand by our motto—'because there's a box, we build and design outside of it." Even though Palmer was a good-looking man and a charmer, his charm was being wasted on the wrong woman. At this point, Abi had little interest in doing anything more than business.

"Abi Trenaulde, line three." They were interrupted by the receptionist's announcement.

"Mr. Stafford, please make an appointment with the receptionist. We have a package put together specifically for the top executives. We would really like to discuss some options with you. Excuse me please." Abi said before exiting the conference room. When she walked away, she could sense his deep warm eyes beaming down at her backside.

She turned. Her assessment was correct. *Surely can't count on a nice-looking gent like that to be on his best behaviour. Married or not, they're all the same*, she thought before picking up the extension on her desk. She set down the manila folder and said into the receiver, "Abi Trenaulde, how may I help you?" She listened to the caller, but her mind wandered to another place. As if a window had opened, a slight breeze entered the room. That familiar fragrance invaded her senses.

"What?" she asked, looking about the room.

"Abi? Is there an issue with what I just said?" the caller questioned.

"No, no. I, um-um. Let me get back to you." Before waiting for a response, she ended the call and placed her head in her hands, resting both elbows on the wooden desk.

Why are you here? she asked herself, but directed her internal thoughts to her imaginary friend. *What did I do to summon your presence?* She paused, waiting for a sign, but there was none, so she asked again, *why are you here*? The manila folder suddenly fell to the floor. *What's that supposed to mean? We vetted this software for months because we need it to start off the company's software development division and now you're having doubts?* For the next thirty minutes or so, Abi had an internal conversation with Roman D'Antonio, and in the end, she determined that he was not pleased with what was about to come.

Chapter v

Throughout his reign, Roman D'Antonio had six wives. After his last divorce, the kingdom was quickly made aware that he was in search of one who would bear his first male heir. His first wife had one surviving birth, a baby girl. He divorced her after the second birth of another daughter who would not survive the delivery. His second wife was infertile. Fearing she had deceived him only to sit by his side, he had her beheaded during a public hearing. His actions sent a message to any other suitors bought to him by dukes and earls in the kingdom. The third wife gave birth to conjoined twin girls, who were locked away in the Tower of Tudor until their demise soon after. His last three wives could only birth daughters. The family was cursed with the inability to birth a male heir to the throne.

"You will not be rid of the D'Antonio curse until you settle the score with your rival family," the elder and Roman's most trusted wise man once warned him.

"How must this be done?" Roman inquired, knowing the family that invaded the country many years prior was killed during the war. Those who weren't killed in battle were rounded up and marched to the tower for beheading.

"The only way of removing the family curse is to wed a descendant from the family who originally placed the curse. She will be the only one that will bring you sons, and many sons you will have with her, and only her. But you have the difficult task of finding her. You are the King of D'Antonio!" The old man bellowed but then respectfully bowed his head and added, "Sir."

For the next eight months, no one in the kingdom laid eyes on the King. He became a reclose in order to bring his new wife into his kingdom to bear his sons. The throne was well protected from attacks by his closest allies. Roman had great faith that not only would they protect the land, they would ensure his peace during this astral transition into another dimension in search of his future wife.

Chapter vi

After the last visit from her imaginary friend, Abi was holed up in her office after going over the agenda for today's meeting with thoughts of her last encounter with Roman D'Antonio. He had appeared after her meeting with Palmer. It was as if she was being scolded like a child for having the slightest attraction to the opposite sex. Earlier she had asked the receptionist to give her some time alone before her next appointment.

The receptionist informed him, "Miss Trenaulde is running slightly late. The previous appointment before you went over its allotted time. Please have a seat and she'll be with you real soon." She smiled before returning her attention back to her phone duties.

"Thanks." Palmer sat near the entrance and retrieved his cell phone. "I just walked in the office but she's tied up at the moment." Palmer spoke quietly into the receiver, but before the conversation took off, Abi appeared in the reception area.

Ignoring the phone glued to his ear, she interrupted his conversation and said, "Sorry to keep you waiting, please follow me. I have some papers for you to look over. You can take them with you so your attorneys can have time to look at them as well. But I'll inform you that the sooner we discuss some open options the sooner our companies can get this over and done with."

After Palmer reviewed her proposed offer to either buyout Virso Pro from DP Tech or join and head-up her software development division, the receptionist buzzed the intercom.

"Miss Trenaulde, if you no longer require my services, I'll be closing the phone lines and leaving for the day."

"That would be fine. Have a good evening and I'll see you in the morning," she said and turned her attention back to Palmer. "I didn't realize it was so late." She paused. "I'm starving." For a moment, a wicked grin appeared across her face. "Would you like to have dinner with me?"

The invitation came as a surprise to Palmer, because up to this point Abi had been all business and hard to read. He couldn't help but wonder if the offer to have dinner was her way of getting to know her future director of software development. Maybe this was her way of thanking him for offering a generous price for exclusive rights to Virso Pro.

"I'd love to," he said calmly while placing the folders inside his briefcase. He smiled at her aggressiveness.

"Wonderful! I hate eating alone. I have a few phone calls to return and wrap up for the day. Why don't you and I meet back here in, let's say, twenty minutes, in the lobby? That way you won't have to carry your things to dinner."

Before leaving the office, Abi freshened her makeup and re-tied her twists in a ponytail atop her head. She engaged in conversation with herself; *Tonight, I'm going to have a nice dinner with a mortal and I'm going to enjoy myself.*

After placing her makeup bag inside her purse, she walked toward the door and turned the knob.

It was locked.

She looked at the knob unsure as to why and when the door had been locked. She tried turning it again, but it didn't budge. This time, Abi knew that for some reason, her fictional friend was holding her hostage. But that would not last long. She turned, balled up both fists and screamed at the top of her lungs, "Roman D'Antonio!" and then between gritted teeth she seethed, "if you don't release this hold, so help me with all the powers I possess, you will regret..."

Before she could get the words out, she was reminded the words her father spoke to her as a child: *'you will need what was handed down to you by our ancestors. As you grow, you will learn how and when to use The Craft.'*

She inhaled that earthy grassy fragrance, he was still there and so was her anger. Abi closed her eyes and counted to ten, attempting to calm her nerves.

When she opened her eyes and turned around, the door slowly opened. She leisurely strolled through it as if nothing at all had happened.

Chapter vii

"Any particular place you were thinking about having dinner?" she asked after seeing Palmer waiting in the reception area. Palmer knew that by the tone of her voice, whomever was on the receiving end of that conversation had gotten their butt chewed off – he assumed she had to have been on a call as she was the only one in the office.

"Other than the hotel restaurant, I don't know any places, so you decide. I'll follow." After exiting the office, the two took the elevator to the underground parking garage. He waited for her activate the keyless entry to a tinted-out seven series BMW. The trunk slowly ascended before she placed her briefcase and handbag inside.

Palmer walked toward the driver's side and opened her door. She smiled while sliding inside. Chivalry was still strong, and he was aware of how to please a woman.

This is a very classy ride for a classy woman. Palmer thought.

They drove the few miles from her office through the city, before she parked in front of an old landmark hotel. Its entrance was spacious with an open atrium. She handed the key to the valet.

After being escorted to an open table, Abi removed the suit jacket, revealing a simple tube top-like blouse with spaghetti straps that showed her perfectly round breasts. Palmer couldn't help but stare at her, towering over her five-foot-three-inch frame like a giant. *Nice petite little thang. I had already checked out this curvy little frame under the layers of fabric covering this perfect shape. Now a brotha can really appreciate those once-hidden curves.* Abi cleared her throat to break him out of his trance.

"Excuse me. I didn't mean to, to; let me get that for you," Palmer stuttered and at the same time reached for her chair. He was slightly embarrassed to be caught staring. Abi sat upright and placed her napkin in her lap.

"I'll have a glass of white wine," she said to the waiter who handed her a menu.

"And you sir?"

"Rum and Coke," he ordered. "I'll have to admit Abi, your CEO is one hell of a—"

"Do you mind if we not discuss business? I make it a rule that after I leave the office all business-related affairs stay within Trenaulde Technology's four walls."

"Fair enough." He responded. *So what will we talk about?* he sarcastically asked himself while burrowing his head inside the oversized menu.

"How long are you going to be in town?" She asked.

"The Trenaulde presentation is the only reason I came to DC. I'm flying back to Atlanta tomorrow morning."

"No sightseeing? You should see the city before you leave." The waiter appeared with their drinks. "Give us a minute," she said to him.

"I'll pass. I saw enough museums when I was younger," Palmer said after the waiter left.

"Can't wait to get back home to the wife." She blushed, which was a first. "Am I being too nosey?"

"No. That question caught me off guard." Abi appeared confused. "I'm not married, Abi." Palmer said while removing the wedding band. "I'm strictly here on business and nothing else. Women tend to flock to a man who isn't wearing a wedding band. It's a decoy."

"Depending on where you are, a man wearing a wedding band could be a magnet for some women. But I can understand that a man as handsome as yourself would have a difficult time keeping the women at bay. And I'm sure you have a nice size heirloom."

"Are you implying that I'm a womanizer? Moi?" he joked.

Abi ignored him and said, "You should try the chef's special. I can promise you, you won't be disappointed." She placed their order once the waiter reappeared, and when he took their order, she continued. "I'm merely stating an obvious fact." This was a woman who knew how to spot a man who had a woman in every city. Palmer hadn't intended to approach her in that manner, and if he were to do so, he needed to devise a different plan in order to move to the next base with her.

"So what about you?" He attempted to even the conversation until he could create an angle. "Are you married? Any kids?"

"I'm single and I have no children."

Somehow, Palmer knew the answer to the question but decided to continue with the conversation. "How did an attractive woman such as yourself managed to remain single?"

"It's easy being single when men are afraid of commitment." For a moment, there was a gleam of sadness in her eyes. Although she had her make-believe friend, he wasn't a real person. Abi had always had the urge to be loved by someone, especially the opposite sex. Her conversation with Palmer was a reminder, and at this moment, that need was beginning to affect her mood.

"Well I'm sure there's a line of drooling brothas jockeying for position on that totem pole."

"You mean the imaginary totem pole. You see, in general, successful women intimidate men. Not intentionally. I've been in this business a very long time, since I was a teenager. Not that I can attest to but I've learned from early on that men can be intimidated by a women with a strong mind." She thought back on her parent's relationship and how her mother was a firm believer in mortality as opposed to her father. She also believed that a successful woman would not be a great suitor for a less than successful man. The waiter appeared with their meal. They ate in silence.

"How about you?" she said between bites of her meal. Palmer stopped eating and looked at her, confused. "Are you intimidated by successful women?"

"Not at all."

She looked at him in disbelief. "Why not? I'm about to acquire a product you worked so feverishly on in the blink of an eye. I control your fate. As I see it, you could be my director of software development or walk away as a millionaire with one stroke of my pen. But we're not going to talk about business, are we?"

He sat upright, wiped his mouth with his napkin and placed it on the table. He paused to contemplate her words. *You can bet your sweet ass I am about to millionaire one way or the other. Even if I don't accept the offer, Trenaulde Technology's competitor is ready and waiting—surely her CEO informed her about their meeting the night of the Expo.*

Everything she said was true, and Palmer was a bit concerned, so he carefully chose his response. "Everything you said has a possibility of becoming true. However, I'm sure Delroy told you about my meeting with your competitor—so because it's business, we're leave that for idle office chat. Am I intimidated because you have this, this, this power in your hands? No. In fact, what I do find intriguing is the beauty you exude, your persuasive business knowledge, and your impressive eye for the minute detail. I am fascinated by your candor." Palmer fought hard to not reach for her hand. There was silence between the two while their eyes searched each other. It appears the two were on the same level and for a moment Abi wanted to smile. She knew at this moment, her new division was in the makings. She finally broke the silence.

"Is there anything else about me that pleases you, Palmer?"

He took another swig of his drink. "You're a very sexy woman. It's very subtle, not in-your-face kind of sexy, but you have just enough synergy to capture the right amount of attention. I like that." Palmer smiled, sensing a slight eruption from below. He shifted in his chair. This conversation was turning him on.

"Sexy?" she chuckled. "That's one hell of way to describe someone in my position, don't you think so? But I've heard it before and it doesn't bother me in the least." Abi lifted her wine glass to him.

Palmer in turn winked at her before taking a large gulp of his drink.

"Wait! Maybe that didn't come out like—"

He was starting to regret using that word 'sexy,' but didn't know how to back out of what he'd said. So instead he allowed her interruption.

"Hmm. Interesting. Now explain to me what makes a man think that a woman is sexy or why did you say that I'm sexy? Huh? Is it money, is it looks? Explain that." Abi had a wicked smile on her face as she took a sip of wine. Truly she was enjoying her evening with this mortal; she also needed to explore more of his behaviour.

"Well if you really want to know, money has nothing to do with a woman being sexy. It's more like what's inside. It's the confidence she has. It's her persona. Being sexy is an attraction to specific qualities a man has for a woman."

"Or a woman has for a man."

"That could be true." Palmer didn't know where the conversation was leading so he chose to listen to what she had to say.

"It is because I can sit here and say I'm looking at a very sexy man. And what makes him sexy is his looks or his smile or the way he smells." Abi was revealing the initial qualities she saw in Palmer when he walked into her office. She was also reflecting on the most important quality she bestowed upon her make-believe friend. His scent was as important to her as his looks. It was important that the two of them could connect by the smell alone. Now she was sitting across from a man, wondering if he wanted more from her. She couldn't tell, as this was her first real date.

Palmer blushed. "What if I were disappointed?" He saw her confusion. "Before you placed our order, you said I won't be disappointed in the meal. What would happen if the meal was disappointing?"

"Then I would have to make sure dessert is at its best." She paused before calling the waiter for the check. "You cleaned your plate so I know you enjoyed it." She had a sultry grin on her face as she signed the check. Then she looked up at Palmer and said, "Now, let's go some place where we both can enjoy a succulent sweetness."

Chapter viii

The two rode from the restaurant through the city practically in silence. Palmer didn't know what to make of the conversation at the restaurant. He thought, *this chick was being flirtatious the whole time, but I am not about to make a move on her even if she were.*

Abi thought, *my first encounter with a real mortal. I hope he's not as complaisant in the bedroom as he seemed to be during our dinner.*

"Where are we?" he asked, looking around. Abi stopped the vehicle in front of an iron gate and waited for it to open. The house and driveway were well lit. Palmer marvelled at the brick exterior home with huge pillars in the front. Then she drove around a circular driveway toward the rear of the home into one of the three-car garages.

"My place. Dessert? Remember?"

He appeared shocked but offered a slight grin. Palmer still didn't want to jump to any conclusions. *Maybe she's going to cook something.* "Wow, I must be special to get an invite to your home." *Yes!* He thought to himself and at the same time simulated a raised triumphant fist. *My prayers were answered. She drove us straight to her place.*

"I'll leave that for you to decide," Abi said after exiting the vehicle. He followed close behind. Once she walked inside the entrance leading into the family room, she ignored the slight pine-like scent that invaded her senses and tossed her jacket on the couch. She assumed her made-up friend was not going to ignore her first encounter with a real live human being. But before she had the chance to fully disrobe, she felt the tug of her top being rolled up and away from her.

Abi sweetheart, you are about to lose whatever you were trying to hold onto. Palmer thought to himself and wasted no time removing her clothing once they got inside. He didn't want to give her any reason to change her mind.

Abi stood nude from the waist up. *There's nothing complaisant about him at all,* she thought.

"Turn around," his baritone voice demanded, unlike the business-like tone heard during their earlier conversation in her downtown office. "Let me look at you." Abi turned and watched him stare at her hardened nipples. She was anticipating his next move and it was a turn-on.

He reached for the waist of the skirt and slid it slowly down her legs. He crouched to remove the skirt. She could feel his warm breath close to her freshly shaved middle. Abi watched him reach for the clip of the garter, releasing its hold on the sheer stockings. Slowly sliding one and then the other onto the top of her heels. He then lifted her legs one by one to remove the shoes and then stockings. Slowly standing, Palmer dropped his suit jacket onto the floor and at the same time began lightly kissing her nipples. She closed her eyes, enjoying his warm moist tongue. She felt herself reaching for the bottom of his shirt, wanting to feel his taut body. When Abi opened her eyes, Palmer had already removed his trousers. She unbuttoned his shirt and slid it down his arms until it too fell to the floor. The two of them stood in the middle of the room, surrounded by discarded clothing. Abi stared at him from top to bottom. She noticed the bulging veins strategically protruding on his toned arms. Her eyes drifted down to his well-defined abdomen. Then her eyes spotted his man-hood, which now stood at attention causing Abi to pause. She was unsure of what else to do.. As if sensing her reluctance, Palmer used both hands pulling her face into his. He began passionately kissing her lips. His moist tongue parted her lips. At that same time, she felt his hands slide down her waist and around her back, his fingers toying at her rear opening. That's when her level of passion heightened. The feeling was heavenly. She had to wrap her arms tightly around his neck to keep from collapsing to the floor but continued nibbling at his tongue as it danced around her mouth. *Ummm,* Abi moaned.

His skilled strokes were causing her excitement to increase. She could feel the moisture gather at first on her face then her entire body appeared wet. She began to feel weak but felt his arms tighten around her backside preventing her from once again losing balance. She could feel the pending climax intensify.

Palmer could tell that Abi wanted him as much as he wanted her, and now he was about to engage in slow, mind-boggling sex meant to drive her passionately insane. Palmer lifted her up onto him, spreading her rear passage to get a better feel of what pleasures he could give.

"Where's your bedroom?" he asked while walking in the direction of where she was pointing. She was too passion-filled to speak correctly.

"Up, straight ahead," she said between kisses. Palmer walked up the circular staircase with her legs tightly wrapped around his waist. Once they were inside her bedroom, the only object he could see was the oversized bed, which was where he deposited her body. Abi reached for him and began stroking his manhood with warm, soft hands. She had never before held such a member in her hands and in awe enjoyed the pleasure she was delivering. Palmer closed his eyes, enjoying her touch. Then he moaned deeply and at the same time reached in his pocket for protection. It wasn't long before she pulled him toward her moistness.

Slowly he entered her warm passage. She was tight but receptive to his deliberate thrust. She wrapped one leg around his waist and began pulling his body into hers. He lifted her other leg up and behind her head to increase the intensity.

After sensing her urgency for more of him, Palmer whispered in her ear, "Aww, you want more of me?" He continued to gently move in a slow rhythm, entering her moistness deeper with each thrust, slowly withdrawing his shaft to the very tip of her wet passage. Palmer kissed the side of her cheek and used his cheek to rub away the moisture that had gathered on hers. He repeated that slow and methodical dance, savoring the warm moistness of her passage. She was on the brink of a climatic explosion with each movement. So was he. But Palmer didn't want this dance to end so soon.

He continued his unhurried thrusts inside of her, aiming for that sweet spot in an orderly movement as her breathing grew louder and louder. Palmer listened to her soft squeals covered in part by his chest. He heard her short, panting breaths, and at the same time, felt the walls of her passage pulsate sporadically around him. He was unable to prolong his physical need to release while being surrounded by her warm, moist vibrating climax. Reaching for her backside, Palmer pushed further and gave her his climax, with loud grunts and moans, in return. Then he collapsed on the bed next to her and gently brought her trembling body into his before kissing her lips. The two cuddled in silence.

ഗഗഗഗ

After about an hour of her sleeping peacefully in his arms, Palmer gingerly slipped from beneath the covers and walked down the stairs to redress. It was after midnight. And as much as he wanted to stay, it was time to leave and prepare for his return home. Another early morning meeting with a customer was scheduled with his partner in Atlanta. He had to make that early morning flight. Using Uber, Palmer requested a ride from his current location to the hotel. Before leaving, he located a piece of paper lying on the end table and scribbled a note.

My sweet Abi,

Thank you for a beautiful evening. That was indeed the best dessert ever. Looking forward to more just like this. ☺

He turned to leave but had not noticed his handwritten note sliding from the end table onto the floor. It was hidden from view.

Chapter ix

After leaving the note on the table for Abi, Palmer smiled to himself because of the evening he spent with her. This had to have been one of, if not the, best evening with a woman he could admit to having in many years, and Palmer hoped that tonight was not the beginning of the end.

Once he exited the double doors of Abi's mansion, they loudly slammed shut behind him, making a booming noise, which caught him by surprise. *What in the hell?* He hoped the noise had not wakened Abi. Palmer shrugged off the offensive manner in which the doors slammed shut and walked toward the iron gate that separated the public roadway from her private property. He located the exit button on the keypad. The car service pulled off the side of the road soon afterwards, and then he could hear the rattle from the gates slamming shut. They too made a loud noise that should have awakened the entire neighborhood. Palmer made a mental note to mention the belligerent noise to Abi.

ovovov

Abi was awakened by the sudden crash of

glass hitting a solid object. She sat upright looking around the dark room. She reached for the light that sat on the nightstand, looking from left to right in search of the object that interrupted her peaceful sleep. The mural that hung above the cedar chest on the opposite side of the room had fallen and shattered onto the wooden object. She scooted to the edge of the bed, slipping her feet inside of her bedroom slippers. Abi walked to where the mural had fallen but noticed through her peripheral vision that some books from the bookshelf were being knocked onto the floor, one after the other.

"Stop it, Roman. You hear me? Stop this right now," she whispered, unaware that Palmer had already left. She turned her attention away from her uninvited guest. "Palmer? Are you in there?" After not receiving a response, Abi opened the bathroom door. It was empty. She walked to where the books had fallen, but before she could bend down to retrieve them, her body was thrown down on her backside and tossed across the room. She slid on the hardwood, stopping at the far wall.

"Dammit! I've had enough of this! What do you want from me? Huh, what do you want?"

Before she could engage in conversation with her friend, the walls began to shake. The plaques above her head were threatening to fall. She looked up and quickly crawled to a safer spot.

Just when she thought this craziness was about to end, her body was slammed violently to the floor, slid across the room of the library, down the long hallway, then through the sitting room and finally in her bedroom, where she was slammed face down in the middle of the bed. She lay there for three hours, unable to move. The apparition hovered over her lifeless body the whole time, unwilling to release his mental hold on her. And then when the alarm clock sounded at 5:45 a.m., he released his powers, giving her back the control he had taken. Abi inhaled a deep breath of air and, panting profusely, sat upright. She sat there attempting to regain her senses. Quickly she ran into the bathroom, turned on the faucet and splashed cold water on her face. Abi stared in the mirror, trying to unravel what had happened to her.

She was confused. Was this a dream? Did her imaginary friend appear last night in her dreams, or did this apparition make his physical presence and why? Her breathing returned to normal, but she was still on edge. Abi had concluded that her make-believe friend was angry with her because she had become physical with a mortal being. Palmer could become a permanent fixture in her life, and if that were to happen, Roman D'Antonio could finally become just a passing phase in her life. Besides, she was far too old to be talking to imaginary friends and concocting fairy tales.

Chapter x

Far away from Brocklehurst, Christians of northern Warwick waged a war on anyone that they felt practiced any form of witchcraft. Even though many accusations were not substantiated, the Parliament did little to protect these accused citizens. Whenever a tragedy occurred in the village, such as the sudden death of one of the rulers, the natives blamed the act on suspicious citizens who were new arrivals to the city. Citizens would gather nightly to decide who practiced magical beliefs. They burned homes and destroyed the lives of many families with these claims. For many years Gaston Trenaulde and his wife practiced The Craft, but they kept to themselves and were rarely seen by the commoners. The Trenaulde families were among the few families who perfected The Craft—the ability to curse their enemy, cast spells, traverse through dimensions. This skill was secret and shared within the family. They managed to avoid being discovered by the citizens by appearing as normal as possible when in the public eye. The two were too sharp and cunning to be found out. But inside their home, their beliefs were on display for all who entered the domain. Soon, the unrest became unbearable, and Gaston knew he had to flee or risk being discovered. Those who could escape sought refuge in neighboring land. The Trenaulde family and many others who were ousted sought refuge in the House of D'Antonio. Gaston's young family eased their way into the kingdom unnoticed by his much younger uncle King Remington and his aging grandmother, Margaret. Even his great uncle Edmund III didn't recognize him. Edmund had become a bitter old man suffering from mental illness. There was no way they would know of his rightful heritage because Gaston was a young lad when his father moved the family to Yorkster. With his return, Gaston had hopes of overthrowing the king, his uncle from the throne and taking over the Kingdom.

Many wars and many generations later, the Trenaulde family was prevented from overthrowing the crown. Those who survived the brutal battles were marched to the Tower of Brocklehurst to meet their untimely death. The Trenaulde family and those from Warwick were shamed due to their failure. But the one thing that remained was the skills they used throughout their reign in Warwick – magical skills Gaston II and Carol had perfected while living away from his family's native land. Their children would practice these skills with their own offspring, who would in turn pass down those same powers to their offspring: the power to cast a spell on anyone at will, as Gaston III had done to the House of D'Antonio just before his beheading.

Chapter xi

In her mind it seemed right at the time; they're both consenting adults. Most women would be feeling guilty about having sex with someone who could become potential employee within company, especially after only knowing him for less than twenty-four hours. But, Abi Trenaulde felt no guilt at all. She did conclude that the sex was satisfying – not in the least like the experience she had with Roman. However, it was probably the best sex any mortal being could perform. What concerned her was the disturbing dream that she had afterwards. She couldn't erase the thought of her imaginary friend being so violent with her. That wasn't the reason for his existence. Her friend had to be a friend and not a bully which is the way Roman D'Antonio behaved that night. She made a mental note to address this behavior at a later time.

That was two nights ago, and now she was staring at a blinking light on the office phone regretting what the caller had to say. DP Tech, Palmer's soon-to-be-defunct company, had been given three business days to respond to their lucrative business offer. This was day two. She clicked the keypad on her laptop and opened a file created for the company.

The receptionist stood by the open door. Abi looked away from the computer screen and stared at her wondering if her experience and professionalism was enough to keep her on, possibly hiring her on as a permanent employee instead of Delroy's niece.

"Hey Abi. Gotta minute?" Delroy peeped his head inside her office.

"What's up?"

"Have you given anymore thought to hiring my niece? I would really like for her to work in a professional environment."

"You asked me that two days ago and my answer hasn't changed. This new temp is working out just fine. I don't see any reason to start over."

At every opportunity, he would practically beg Abi to hire his niece. But Abi was strongly against hiring family members. This new temp would be her excuse for not hiring Delroy's family member.

"Miss Trenaulde, DP Tech is holding on line two." That was her second attempt to get Abi to pick up on the flashing line. She was stalling, answering his call as long as possible.

This time you're going to have to wait for my response, Abi thought.

After several long minutes, Abi finally picked up the receiver and said calmly in as professional tone as one could muster, "This is Miss Trenaulde, how may I help you?"

"Good morning Miss Trenaulde. This is Eli Glenn, I represent DP Tech." She emitted a slight sigh, not yet prepared to have a conversation with Palmer. "We'd like to meet and discuss the package your company put together and propose a few options to your plan."

"Mr. Glenn, Trenaulde Technology will listen to whatever options DP Tech has formulated based on our findings. However, according to our attorneys, the package is fair and complete. Also, please keep in mind that the longer this deal is on the table, the more likely the offer will be rescinded. You may make an appointment with my secretary. In the meantime, have a good day, sir," she stoically said and transferred the call to the receptionist. "Please schedule some time later in the week with DP Tech." Then she disconnected the call. *The nerves of him having his attorney call me. He should have at least awakened me before leaving.*

Abi was contradicting herself; part of her wanted to hear his voice, but the other side of her didn't want to deal with the emotions she was experiencing. Whatever the case, she had every intention of making him pay for having someone else do his dirty work. She sat upright, folded her arms on the desk and stared. *Maybe it was too soon and he didn't want to deal with my wrath. And to add insult to injury, they want to propose options to my offer.* Abi knew she wanted to acquire DP Tech because of their latest product currently being marketed to the Department of Defense. She had plans of adding Virso Pro under Trenaulde Technology's Software Development Division.

The receptionist stuck her head in. "Miss Trenaulde, DP Tech and their attorneys are

House of D'Antonio

scheduled for tomorrow morning at 10am."

"How can that be?" Abi asked while scanning her planner. "I have to attend the reception at the mayor's building at 10 o'clock. And did you consult with our attorneys?" She spat.

"Yes I did and the reception was cancelled yesterday, remember? There was an issue with the inspection, something about it not getting finalized."

"Close the door behind you," she said and turned her attention back to the file she had previously opened. Instead, a message indicator showed that she had new e-mail in her Inbox.

Once she opened the application, the subject line read:

YOU BELONG TO ME

She stared at the screen, her mouth wide open. There was neither a Sender nor Recipient associated with the e-mail message. Suddenly, the laptop slammed shut. It startled her, causing Abi to jump backwards. "What the…" before she could complete the sentence her door flung opened and violently slammed against the doorjamb. Abi slowly walked toward the door and peeped down the narrow passage.

The receptionist lifted her head and smiled. "Do you need something Miss

Trenaulde?"

Abi ignored her and closed the door. "Roman." she whispered, and then waited for a sign of acknowledgement that wasn't there.

Angry, Abi sat at her desk and summoned her imaginary friend. *Okay Roman, it's you and me.* She looked around and waited. Then that familiar grassy, pine-like fragrance invaded her senses. He was there. Staring straight ahead, she thought, *you're not real. You're a fictional character. A character I created when I was a child!* Then she said out loud, "So therefore, know that I can make you go away."

Chapter xii

The attorney representing Trenaulde Technology, and the attorney representing DP Tech along with Palmer Stafford, were led into the conference room. Abi had informed the receptionist to buzz her once they were seated. Delroy waited with Abi inside her office. She had hired him shortly after incorporating the company and Delroy had been invaluable throughout his tenure. The fifty-eight-year-old had retired from the federal government with over thirty-five years experience. Thus far, Abi was pleased with the business he brought to the company. This venture was going to be a great addition to the company.

Ten minutes before their scheduled time, the receptionist buzzed the line.

"Good morning. I'm Abi Trenaulde." She watched the men stand once she appeared, and then introduced her CEO.

DP Tech's attorney greeted the pair in a polite tone. He then introduced his client—as if neither of them had met Palmer before this meeting. The two men shook hands, Palmer smiled at Abi.

Without any acknowledging of his smile, Abi said, "Palmer Stafford. Nice to see you once again." But she avoided Palmer's outstretched hand and walked toward the opposite side of the table.

They listened as the two attorneys rattled off a slew of questions regarding Trenaulde Technology's offer, presented during the first meeting. Abi took the time to explain the pros of joining the company and the direction the new division was headed. Trenaulde Technology's CEO answered questions regarding the offer. Before ending the presentation, the attorney representing Trenaulde Technology excused himself after leaving copies of the presentation for each attendee.

By the time the four-hour meeting ended, everyone was exhausted, but most if not all of the details were finalized. The attorney agreed to conduct a second meeting just to iron out the legalities of the offer. Abi smiled internally, knowing the offer was fair but saw the unpleasant look on Palmer's face. The two watched the CEO gather his things before leaving them alone in the room. Abi was finally alone with Palmer. DP Tech's attorney argued not only for a division within the company, which was in the original offer but he also wanted a seat on Trenaulde Technology's board of Directors and additional stock options. Trenaulde Technology's attorney refused to give in to any additional demands citing their offer was generous enough.

"Palmer, you seem a bit unhappy with the offer." She leaned back in her chair.

"I guess you think I should be jumping with joy, but I was hoping your attorney could sweeten the deal a little." he leaned into her. "Abi, I'm looking forward to running the software division because I know how to build and design for the future, however I also know my product. I at least deserve a seat on the board." His piercing eyes dug into her like embers surrounding a fire. She stared back at him, fighting back the smirk.

Abi thought before speaking, *I hope you think twice about the next time you make love to me and then leave without so much as a goodbye kiss.*

"Let me break it down to you like this." She leaned forward. This time it was her with piercing eyes, digging into Palmer's. "I know what you can do; I know the value of your product. Delroy couldn't stop talking about it after the demo, but it's not at all a bad deal. As a matter of fact, I think it's very lucrative for you." She was going to get her way in this deal, one way or another. She always did, and this was not her first. She wanted to have Palmer signed onto Trenaulde Technology by mid-year to run that part of the company. "You're getting a large signing bonus, a lucrative payoff for your Virso Pro software, a six-figure salary, and fringe benefits offered to all of our directors.

Palmer finally spoke. "These a great perks presented but I was hoping we could negotiate additional terms to your offer. But hey, I guess we both win in the long run."

"You're a smart man Palmer, Delroy spoke highly of you after your first meeting with him. Besides, an offer such as this doesn't come around often. Listen to your attorney." She gathered her papers and before walking out of the room added, "And if you think my competitor can match or beat any offer that was mentioned in this room, you are a fool."

Palmer was perplexed by her last comment. He had an odd feeling that maybe she was having regrets about becoming physical with him so soon. But it seemed as if the two of them were compatible. Maybe he was wrong but that night everything about Abi Trenaulde felt right and he was looking forward to leading her newly created division – he was also hoping to pick up where they left off.

Chapter xiii

As soon as the door closed shut, he pulled out his cell phone and quickly dialed his attorney. Before he spoke, Palmer asked, "What in the hell did we get ourselves into?" Palmer was unsure of who the woman was that just left the room.

"I knew she would be a hard one to sell when I first spoke with her on the phone. You didn't say she was a hound dog." his attorney said.

"She didn't build this empire by being a pushover, either." Palmer whispered into the receiver.

"At the rate that mouth was running, someone needs to give her a good stiff one," Eli stated. Palmer chose not to comment because maybe it was that good stiff one that he had given her last week that caused this fiasco.

"It's not a bad thing but I was hoping to get more out of the deal."

Well, we gave it our best and Palmer, it really is a good deal—better than you can get from anyone else. So forget about Defense and that other company for now." his attorney told him.

He exited the conference room deep in conversation with his attorney, so deep that Palmer was unaware that he was being watched.

ᎧᏉᎧᏉᎧᏉ

Once the door to the hotel room slammed shut, Palmer called Trenaulde Technology. He didn't want anyone to know about his sexual rendezvous with Abi. His attorney would clearly be upset this time with everything that has transpired and that Palmer could have caused this offer to backfire.

"Abi Trenaulde, please," he stated once

the receptionist answered. After a long pause, the call was answered.

"I'm sorry but Miss Trenaulde is gone for the day." It was five o'clock in the afternoon; businesspeople didn't leave at normal hours, at least not Abi. He had the thought of returning to her office. But instead he chose to stay put. *If I show up at her office and she's not there, like the receptionist said, then it could look bad for me.* The last thing he needed to do was to make a fool of himself by showing up unannounced.

Ten minutes later, there was a faint tap on his hotel room door. She stood on the opposite side and clutched her Italian bag.

"Are you going to invite me in?"

He was bewildered, surprised to see her standing at his hotel room door.

"Well?" she asked again, but instead of waiting for an answer, Abi strutted passed him. He watched her drop her bag on the tiny table, and then she removed her jacket, laying it on the armrest.

"I'm not sure I understand your game?"

"Well, let me explain it to you. What I do is my business and not the business of my company, my partner or anyone else. When I'm in the office, I'm there to conduct business and not bullshit. So don't expect me to play footsie with you under the table." Abi walked toward him and begin unbuttoning his shirt. Palmer unzipped the skirt she was wearing, letting it fall to the floor.

"There's nothing wrong with a little footsie to ease some of the tension."

"I have other ways of relieving the tension." Abi walked toward the bed and sat. She placed her bended knee on the edge. She wasn't wearing panties.

As if programmed to do so, Palmer dropped to his knees between her legs. Admiring her shaved middle, he took hold of both legs and slid her toward the edge. He kissed both sides of her passage before planting light kisses on her middle. Abi rested on the bed enjoying the delight in receiving his passionate kisses. After hearing her moans of pleasure, Palmer began licking her entire middle from the front to her rear passage. Abi's entire body started to shake; she had never experienced this new high her body was receiving. The more Palmer pushed his tongue in and out of her rear passage the louder her moans became. Only seconds after that, her juices exploded. He continued to lightly suck on her until her moans subsided. Palmer stood, placed a knee on the bed, straddled her and lifted her limp body toward the middle of the bed. She moaned and wrapped the blanket around her body, turning away from him.

He kissed her on the shoulder and whispered, "I'm hungry."

She felt his hardness pressed against her backside. "You just ate."

"I need some more, you know some tension relief."

There was an awkward pause before Abi slid from the blanket and begin redressing. She smiled, "That's not going to happen."

Because he was checking out of the hotel in less than an hour so that he could take a cab to National Airport, he didn't argue. What he did do was flop backwards on the bed and clutch his manhood. Even though her visit was unexpected, it was welcome. Palmer wished he could finish with some earth-shattering sex, but the oral he performed for her would have to suffice.

He sat on the bed watching her every move. "The next time, I guess I'll need to be better prepared for your surprise visits, huh?"

Abi ignored him, not in the least concerned about his temper tantrum. She reached for her handbag and jacket, and then walked out of the hotel room, allowing the door to slam shut.

Chapter xiv

The next day after returning to Atlanta, Palmer had signed all the necessary papers needed to transfer his copyrights of Virso Pro software to Trenaulde Technology. He also signed a non-compete agreement with the company and was ready to begin his new position as Director of Software Development.

He reclined in the oversize chair in his

office and thought, *with the bonus, company vehicle,*

and the payout for the software copyrights; I need to

take a vacation.

What caught him by surprise is the email

he received from the CEO of Trenaulde

Technology.

```
To: P. Sheldon
From: D. Myers
Subject: New Software Development
Division Celebration
Palmer,
Please join us in celebrating the
opening of our new division soon
to be operating in the Atlanta
office. See attached flyer for the
location, date, and time
Please feel free to forward this
email to your staff.
```

ovovov

Palmer smiled before sending back

his response, which read: My staff and I will love to attend this celebration.

VVVV

At five twenty, Palmer and two close friends walked inside the Georgian Room at the Ritz Carlton Hotel. Immediately, he scanned the room in search of any familiar faces, especially Abi. He spotted Delroy standing by the bar with a drink in his hand. Palmer walked to wear he stood and the two men shook hands. He then introduced his two friends who were only there for support.

"You're looking at two of the

brightest men in software development I know. Now, if I can convince these two to join me, I want them by my side in this software division."

The two men smiled in acknowledgement of the compliment.

They were introduced to other employees from Trenaulde Technology, but Palmer had all but lost interest, as he had not yet spotted the one person he couldn't wait to see.

Abi had taken a later flight than the rest of the team so she arrived at Hartsfield-Jackson airport. By the time she checked in the room, she was exhausted but decided to shower and dress for the celebration. Deep down, she was looking forward to seeing Palmer once again.

When she walked inside the Georgian Room she immediately spotted Palmer in conversation with a young lady she didn't recognize. Abi felt a slight hint of jealousy after seeing Palmer seemingly enjoying the conversation. She dismissed those feelings and walked to where Delroy stood.

"Nice crowd. How's it going?" She smiled and ordered a drink from the bartender.

He didn't notice her walk in the room but out of the corner of his eye, Palmer spotted Abi near the bar engaged in conversation with Delroy. He wanted to end the conversation he was having with this person who was obviously showing more interest in him than he in her.

Once the celebration started to whine down, Palmer found himself standing in a corner nursing a rum and coke. Abi had been mingling with other employees through out the evening. He decided that this would be his last drink before calling it a night.

"Palmer," she taped his shoulder to get his attention. He turned and smiled, happy to finally be acknowledged. "Did you enjoy yourself tonight?"

"It's good to see you Abi."

"Delroy said you've started recruiting developers already. So I guess that means you're excited to start as our new director."

"Something like that."

She smiled. "I took a later flight and am exhausted." Abi paused, looked around the room and then added, "I'm in the Presidential suite if you'd like to join me for a nightcap." She turned and walked out of the room.

Palmer watched her exit the room, took the final gulp from his glass, placed it on the table and walked out of the room. He was smitten with Abi and accepted her invitation without hesitation.

Once inside the room, Abi handed him two small bottles from the mini-bar and excused herself. When she returned she was dressed in a T-shirt and shorts. He handed her a mixed drink and removed his tie.

She took a sip from the glass and said, "Even though I'm exhausted, I'm really glad to have your company tonight."

"Here, let me take this," Palmer said while reaching for her drink. He placed both glasses on the nightstand, reclined on the king-sized bed and pulled her body into his. They slept that way the entire night.

That next morning she told him, "You do not have to take me to the airport. It's much easier for me to take a taxi, Palmer."

"No. I want to take you and see you off." Abi was a bit concerned that Delroy or someone else from the company may notice the two either leaving the hotel or together at the airport.

He wouldn't take no for an answer so while at the airport, Palmer checked her bags with the skycap and reached for her hand.

"Palmer, as much as I enjoy you, I'm concerned about being seen like this with you."

Pulling her into him, Palmer lowered his head, placing his forward on hers and said, "Goodbye Abi." Then he let go of her hand and watched her walk through the sliding doors.

Chapter xv

After that last conversation in her office with her make-believe friend, Abi felt her point was made. She hadn't had an impromptu visit from Roman. One day she would conjure his presence but for now, it was time she put an end to his frequent visits.

She sat upright in the middle of her bed reviewing some of the legal briefs presented by

Trenaulde Technology's attorneys. The deal was all set, and she was excited to put all the legalities behind her and focus on her new division with Palmer as her new director.

Abi thought back to their encounter last night at the celebration and this morning. His actions at the airport showed her that Palmer was truly having feelings for her and maybe she was also falling for him. She blushed as a tingly feeling traveled down her spine. She would have Delroy meet monthly with all of the division directors together to discuss their individual status. *That's one way of spending time together, she thought.*

She was startled after hearing a loud crash coming from the room next to her office. Abi couldn't see what caused the commotion, so she slid out of bed and walked in the direction of where she heard the noise. She saw nothing unusual, and nothing appeared to be out of place. She shrugged it off and went back to her reading. Once she got situated, something forced her onto her back. She couldn't move. The room went dark, and even the light from the full moon failed to illuminate the room. But the one thing that was clear was the scent she had created long ago had returned; that grassy, pine-like fragrance made just for her imaginary friend. Just when she thought he had gotten the message, Roman D'Antonio made his presence once again.

"Roman D'Antonio!" She managed to say but was still pinned to the center of the king-size bed. "Let me go!"

Never! The entire room seemed to vibrate after the apparition mentally transported that one declaration. Slowly and methodically, he continued his demand. *Leave this mortal land and come with me to my eternal kingdom.*

Her eyes began to blink rapidly after feeling this ghostly being moved closer to her limp body. She had no control over what would occur next. Abi then felt her nightgown slide down her shoulders and away from her. She lay nude, feeling the weight of the ghostly intruder resting on top of her. She felt his breath on every inch of her. It was warm and satisfying. She almost felt a bit of shame from appreciating the pleasure being imposed on her by her make-believe apparition. She couldn't resist the powerful sensation of having this indistinguishable imaginary being massaging her body like no other before. It was a feeling of pending ecstasy that seemed to last longer and be much more powerful than any she had felt. The bed shook violently, shaking her from side to side. The walls begin to close in on her, and Abi was on the verge of losing consciousness. But before passing out, her mind lapsed into a dream-like state. She felt calm and tranquil. Her soul soared toward the ceiling and hovered over her physical body that remained motionless on the bed. Abi tried to will her soul back inside of her body, but the energy to pull her soul away was much greater than the energy to return. Roman's powers were beckoning her soul toward him. Abi was being led away from her physical body, away from the bed, away from her home. Abi's soul raced through the night skies, across the moon and stars. She was moving at a fast pace, toward something unfamiliar to her—another place in time. Her soul had soared to some unknown place and time.

Chapter xvi

Before her stood a six-foot-tall masculine figure of a man wearing a long, fur-like robe draped about his shoulders. The length of it hung well past the platform where he stood. His headgear was covered with gemstones from front to back, top to bottom. He wore armor similar to that of a knight, but he was far from it – he was the leader of these people. Her senses kicked in and once again the grassy, pine-like fragrance she created years ago had returned. She stared up at his unshaven face. The colors he wore spoke royalty. The man's face was gorgeous. His deep dark eyes seemed to be piercing through hers. His dark hair hung down his shoulders. Abi was taken aback by his commanding appearance.

Somehow she projected herself through time to the world where her imaginary friend originated. Or did he kidnap her soul to bring her here with him, here in this ancient land. This same world she created as a child has now stolen her from time and placed her in this ageless land. *But how can this be happening? I made you up*, she thought. Abi looked around and saw several women sat at Roman's feet with bowed heads, not daring to look at him. Behind him were thousands of warriors carrying shields and crossbows. They looked regal and honored to serve him. Abi looked past the thousands of armored men and scanned the land surrounding them. She saw two tall towers, château's in the valley, a large sculpture fountain with water flowing down, several stoned pathways leading up towards a huge palace lined with immaculate and well maintained landscape. It was a beautiful site.

He extended a hand to her, but she refused

it and chose to stare at her own attire. She thought back on the moment right before her soul released itself from her physical body—her nightgown had been removed. And now Abi was dressed in a long Celtic chemise with oversized sleeves. On top of it was an even longer, dark, maiden sleeveless dress, tied tightly at the midsection. *Where am I?* She looked around the coliseum for answers but then looked at the extended hand. She stared at him before speaking. "Who are you?"

"Ruler of the Brocklehurst Kingdom, Head of the House of D'Antonio. I am King Roman D'Antonio. Take my hand and live forever with me in this land amongst my people. As my queen, you will bare many son's who will sit on the D'Antonio throne."

The words from her father replayed in her mind as it has so often done in the past: *'you will need what was handed down to you by our ancestors. As you grow, you will learn how and when to use The Craft.'*

Abi wondered if this is the moment she should have used The Craft? She wondered if her Silver Cord, her energetic link to travel back home was still attached from her soul to her physical body. It would serve as her energy source to return—if that were to be her decision. For Abi this would be a difficult decision to decide whether to leave such a wealthy land, a throne, this euphoric feeling of peace and tranquility. Once again she looked at his outreached hand and this time extended hers.